THE SUSPECT'S WIFE

MICHAEL KINGSWOOD

Copyright © 2012 by Michael Kingswood

Cover Art Copyright © Jose Antonio Sánchez Reyes | Dreamstime.com

ISBN 13: 978-1-950683-25-3

ISBN 10: 1-950683-25-7

This story is a work of fiction. Names, characters, places, and incidents are either products of the author's imagination or used fictitiously. Any resemblance to actual events, locales, or persons, living or dead, is entirely coincidental.

All rights reserved.

No part of this book may be reproduced in any form or by any electronic or mechanical means, including information storage and retrieval systems, without written permission from the author, except for the use of brief quotations in a book review.

Parties interested in licensing rights to this property, should contact publisher@ssnstorytelling.com.

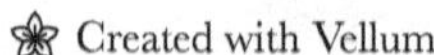 Created with Vellum

Contents

About This Book

A client's cryptic story leads Private Investigators Ronald Harper and Kathleen Davidson to evidence of multiple murders.

The Suspect's Wife is a 9,200 word short mystery.

Enjoy the book! After you're done, please come to Michael's website and sign up for his mailing list at michaelkingswood.com/newsletter-signup/. Guaranteed to be spam free, he uses it to announce new releases and special promotions for his fans.

The Suspect's Wife

R onald Harper shut the door of his car, a late model Outback that was painted a shade of blue so dark most people thought it was black, and thumbed the remote on his keychain. The squawk of the doors locking elicited a slight smile, as it always did. It was good to get around in style.

The early autumn morning was cool, but not uncomfortable, as he walked the hundred yards from the parking lot to his office building. It was almost not worth wearing his leather jacket, but the weather guessers had predicted a cold front was going to roll in later in the day, maybe bringing rain with It. And besides, he had an image to maintain.

The simple swinging door pulled open easily. Kathleen must already be inside; she was the only other person who had a key. Hardly a surprise. She was far more a morning person than he. With a wry grin, Ronald let the door swing shut behind him and took the narrow staircase beyond two at a time. As always, by the time he reached the top, he felt more energetic. Nothing like getting the blood pumping to wake a fellow up.

The staircase ended at a wood door that contained a translucent window in its upper half. The words, "Davidson and Harper, Private Investigators" were stenciled into the window in black tape.

Home sweet home.

He pushed the door open and walked into the familiar office. He instantly felt his mood improve. There was something about the dark-stained wood panelling on the walls, the weathered leather couch off to one side, his and Kathleen's desks against the back wall, the narrow window between them that looked out onto the river, the smell of leather, paper, cigarettes, and secrets that made him feel comfortable.

He grinned at Kathleen as he entered and received her usual half-smirk in response.

"Ron. Out late with Isabel again?"

He shrugged. "Not too late. She had an early meeting today." He stepped around the coffee table in front of the couch and circled around to his desk chair. It was pricey. Ergonomically precise, or so the salesman said. Whatever. It was the most comfy office chair Ronald had ever sat in, and was worth every penny. "Anything brewing?"

Kathleen shook her head. "Just the coffee." She raised her mug to her lips and took a drink before adding, "Which is running low, by the way. It's your turn to buy."

Ronald nodded. He didn't need her to remind him of that. But then, she was the one for details. It showed from the way she dressed. Always an impeccable business suit. Whether with pants or a skirt, she always looked her best. This morning, she wore dark blue; he noted she seemed to wear blue more often than not. Probably because it set off her eyes well. She was not his type; he generally did not prefer blondes. And even if he had, she was his partner, not a potential hookup. But all the same, he had to admit she always managed to look good.

Ronald chuckled inwardly as he wondered how many of their clients signed on because of how she looked even more than their firm's reputation as a top-notch investigating unit. She would probably rip his heart out if he suggested it, but he could think of at least two in the last month who had only come around after meeting them….her…in person. A lesser man would feel slighted for that, but whatever brought in the cash sat well with Ronald.

"We've got a ten o'clock."

Ronald glanced at the clock. Nine fifty.

"What's the deal?"

Kathleen shrugged. "Some kind of family trouble, from the sound of it."

Great. Another job chasing after some bimbo's husband, trying to get pictures of him in the act with the "other woman". Sometimes it turned out they really were fooling around, but Ronald was almost always appalled by the women those guys chose as mistresses. If you're going to risk your marriage and screw up your financial future, at least go for someone hot! But no, a lot of the time those guys hooked up with fat trolls. No accounting for some men's thought processes, he supposed.

"Well at least it's a pay check." Ronald tried to put more cheeriness into his voice than he thought.

Kathleen snorted.

Fifteen minutes passed quickly. A cup of coffee and the morning paper saw to that. But by a few minutes after ten, Ronald began to get annoyed. Maybe it was the Marine Corps refusing to let him go, but people who were not punctual were very…

A firm knock on the door broke Ronald's chain

of thought. He looked up and saw a man silhou-
etted beyond the translucent glass. He exchanged
glances with Kathleen, then stood and pulled the
door open.

And was just about bowled over as the man
shoved his way into the room. He was not overly
tall, about Ronald's height, but he was broad, with
the shoulders of a linebacker and the musculature
to match. His face was round and dominated by a
hooked nose that almost made one not notice the
thin, almost feminine lips around his mouth. He
had black hair that hung limply to his eyebrows in
front and was cut short in back. He dressed simply,
in jeans - Levi's Ronald noted - and a plain white t-
shirt beneath a maroon windbreaker.

As the man swept past, Ronald recovered his
balance and pushed the door closed. He flipped
the deadbolt and pulled the roll-up curtain that
hung at the top of the door's window down, then
turned back toward the man. Or rather, his back.

The man had eyes only for Kathleen. "Ms.
Davidson?" he asked. His voice was a high bari-
tone, almost a tenor, which did not fit with his
hulking form very well at all. He sounded nervous.

Kathleen smiled winningly at him and rose
from her desk chair. "Good morning, Mr. Samuelson." She extended her hand and he shook it
quickly, as though as an afterthought. "This is my
partner, Ronald Harper."

The man, Samuelson, blinked and looked aside
toward Ronald as though seeing him for the first
time. And no wonder, the way he had barged in.
He swallowed and managed an apologetic smile.
"Nice to meet you." He did not offer his hand to
shake.

"Likewise," Ronald said. He returned to his
desk and leaned back against its front edge, folding

his hands over his chest. This client was not very impressive so far. "What can we do for you, Mr. Samuelson?"

Samuelson opened his mouth, then paused. He looked away from Ronald, toward the door and for a moment Ronald thought he was going to flee. Then he swallowed and spoke, his eyes still directed elsewhere.

"I think someone killed my wife."

RONALD GAZED through his binoculars at a little house on a hill. It was the only building for miles. No surprise there. It had taken forty-five minutes on the Interstate to get there from town. As always, he was amazed how quickly civilization faded once one got outside the city limits and past the suburbs.

The house was simple: square-shaped, painted white with a shingle roof. It had a small porch out front and a meandering driveway that disappeared in the trees as it descended the hill. Its address placed it on the road Ronald was parked on the side of, which meant either the road curved mightily as it approached the hill or the driveway was excessively long. He was betting on the later.

"That surely doesn't look like the scene of a grizzly crime," he mused. That much was certain. Ronald was quite sure when he and Kathleen got up there they would find nothing more interesting than an old lady with her cats, or at best a country couple who preferred to be alone now that the kids had flown the coop. Certainly not a cold-blooded killer. "Ten to one she just ran off with some guy and Samuelson's making things up in his own mind."

On the seat next to him, Kathleen smirked but said nothing.

"And why the hell didn't he go to the cops if he thought…" Ronald stopped talking. He did not need to finish that thought to know the answer. Sometimes you needed justice, not law. And so you don't go to the cops. But in those times, people generally take matters into their own hands, not hire PIs.

He rolled his eyes. The hell with it. It was a paycheck. Not that he was going to kill anyone; if it was what Samuelson thought, Ronald intended to call the cops himself quick as can be. It was Samuelson's problem if he needed to spend a bunch of money so that someone else could make the call, not him.

"You set?"

Kathleen nodded. "Just waiting on you."

Ronald chuckled and put the Outback in gear.

The driveway was every bit as long, and quite a bit more steep, as it appeared from down below, but eventually they pulled out from underneath the gold and red of leaves that were getting ready to fall and emerged in the small yard in front of the house.

Up close, the house was quite a bit less appealing that it had been from afar. The paint was peeling in many places. One of the shutters on the front windows was knocked askew. And the roof was in dire need of re-shingling. Weeds grew tall in the remains of a flower bed below the front porch, and it looked as though the owners had not mowed the lawn in a week.

"Nice place," Kathleen said, her tone more than a little ironic, as they exited the car.

Ronald was forced to agree.

He took a moment to verify his Glock was sitting properly in its holster in the small of his back, then he set off toward the house. Kathleen followed at his right. She, like Ronald, was constantly scanning the area, her expression wary but not nervous. He noticed, though, that her left hand never strayed far from her hip, where she wore her piece on a holster at her waist, beneath her light jacket.

The steps leading to the front porch creaked slightly as Ronald stepped up, and for a moment he pictured himself breaking through and falling hip-deep through a hole just large enough for one leg. The thought of such a ridiculous predicament lent extra speed to his stride, and the step did not give way anyway. All the same, when he reached the top it was with just a tiny bit of relief.

Kathleen looked at him askance. "You alright?"

He spread his hands and grinned for a second, nodding.

Her sniff spoke volumes.

The front door was, once upon a time, painted red and inlaid with a brass knocker. But, like everywhere else on the house, the paint was peeling, revealing the underlying wood. And it looked as though no one had polished the brass in decades, it had so much verdigris. Narrow windows stood on either side of the door, running its entire length, but the view inside was obscured by drab-looking hanging drapes.

The only sound was the noise of his and Kathleen's breathing, and the rustle of the breeze through the tree limbs back at the clearing's edge.

"Something's not right here," Ronald said. "Didn't Samuelson say someone lives here? I'd say we're the first people to set foot on this porch in a year."

Kathleen did not reply at first, instead moving to the right, toward another window, longer like the kind people mount in their living rooms. Ronald could see from where he was the glass was cracked in several places. She looked through it for a short moment, then glanced back at him.

"I don't see any movement." The same doubt he felt had crept into her voice. What sort of half-assed wild goose chase had Samuelson set them on?

Ronald and Kathleen traded looks. He was half-inclined to just say "Screw it" and go home, but he could tell from Kathleen's expression she would have none of that. And she had a point; Samuelson had paid them a retainer, after all. But still...

"Alright, let's get it done," he said with resignation.

Ronald stepped up to the door, his right hand slipping behind his back to grasp the grip of his Glock. To his side, Kathleen also made ready to draw. He glanced back at her, and she nodded.

Ronald knocked, a quick powerful staccato that should have been clearly audible throughout the house.

After what seemed like forever, but in fact was only a minute when Ronald checked his watch, there was neither an answer at the door nor any sound from within.

He knocked again. Still nothing. It looked like they had to do it the hard way. He hated the hard way.

Ronald stepped back and made a sweeping gesture from Kathleen toward the door. "You're up," he said. She was the locksmith of their pair, not he.

Kathleen rolled her eyes, but got down to business without commenting. Her expression said enough.

She retrieved a set of tools from the inner

pocket of her jacket and crouched down before the doorknob. As Ronald kept watch, both on the interior of the house and the yard and tree line, she fiddled around with a pair of long, needle-like implements. After a few brief moments poking and prodding, there was an audible CLICK.

Nodding in satisfaction, Kathleen replaced the tools and straightened. She rolled her shoulders slowly then drew her Sig Sauer. Ronald did not say how awkward the large weapon looked in her small hands. She would kick his ass for that, and besides he knew well that she was a crack shot with it. Instead, he drew his Glock and assumed a ready stance.

Kathleen glanced back at him and he nodded. At his signal, she pulled the door open and he charged through.

The inside of the house was dim, dusty, and filled with unpleasant smells: mildew, but beneath that a rank odor that he could not place though it nagged at him. The door opened into the living room, which was sparsely filled with a couple chairs and a small couch, all of which were covered in cloth, as though the owner had closed up the house for the season. That had to have been a number of seasons ago, though, as a thick layer of dust covered everything.

"Classy place," Ronald muttered.

He stalked over to the sole exit from the room: a doorway that was filled with hanging beads that had long since lost their luster. The hallway beyond led left to a pair of bedrooms and a bathroom, and right to a kitchen. All were as sparsely furnished and dust-filled as the living room. Except for the kitchen.

"Well look at what we have here," Kathleen said as the pair surveyed the scene.

The kitchen was L-shaped, with counters containing a sink and an electric stove along the rear wall of the house. On the wall opposite stood a refrigerator alongside extensive cabinets and shelving. At the bend of the L lay a breakfast nook complete with a table and chairs which stood before a bay window that overlooked the downslope of the hillside and the valley below. A windowed door to the left of the table led to the back yard. To the table's right, at the end of the L, was a moderate sized alcove where a pot rack hung next to a baker's rack, which stood next to a closed door. The room was painted a cheerful yellow, with paintings of flowering vines curling around every corner and along the edge of the ceiling. The floor was ceramic tile and the countertops granite. Overall, a well put-together kitchen.

And it was immaculate. Not a trace of dust dirtied the room, in stark contrast with the rest of the house. Clearly someone had been here. Often. Why would they only frequent the kitchen, and not the rest of the house?

"Looks like they've been using the back door," Kathleen said, crouching down near that door and examining the lock. "It's not been jimmied."

"Hmm. I wonder where..." Ronald turned the knob on the door near the baker's rack and pulled it open. The door creaked softly; the hinges required some WD-40. Beyond, a set of rickety stairs descended into darkness. The cellar.

Ronald looked back at Kathleen, who pursed her lips for a moment in thought. Finally she shrugged. "Might as well."

They went down slowly, Ronald leading the way. A lone lightbulb dangled from the ceiling, providing dim illumination to the stairs, but after about a dozen steps, they turned left and that small illumination was mostly lost.

Ronald slowed, flexing his fingers on the grip of his Glock as his eyes adjusted to the suddenly increased gloom. Ahead, he could vaguely make out the outline of an empty doorframe. Beyond was only shadow. This was not going to do at all. He stopped and reached into the inner pocket of his leather jacket where he always carried a penlight. There was certainly another light around somewhere, but damned if he wanted to fumble around in the darkness until he found it.

The beam of his penlight caught details here and there. A desk against the wall with a bulletin board hanging above it. A chest of some sort in the corner. A bed - a cot? - In the other corner. Another door?

And then the lights came on, making Ronald blink at the sudden glare. Acting on instinct, he leapt to the right and dropped into a crouch, Glock rising to firing position as he spun around.

And saw Kathleen standing just inside the doorway, he fingers on the light switch right next to the doorway and a bemused expression on her face.

"Christ!" Ronald muttered as he lowered the Glock and stood up straight.

Kathleen shook her head and chuckled. "Why so jumpy, Ron? I mean really..." Her words drifted off and her eyes widened.

Ron turned, following her gaze to the bulletin board. What he saw there sent a chill running down his spine.

GREGORY BARNES WAS every bit the cliché

homicide detective. From the cheap suit to the bad tie to the constant scowl and the "I think I'm a tough guy" attitude. Ronald hated him on sight. Problem was, he was stuck with him.

Had they discovered the items in the cellar back in town, Ronald had a number of contacts in the Department he could call to grease the skids, or at least edit the official report so that he and Kathleen would not be mentioned in it, or bothered by it. Out here in the boonies, though...

"You want to tell me why in the hell you didn't call us as soon as you got done talking with your client?" Jesus, Barnes even *sounded* like a guy from a bad cop show.

Ronald sat in one of the interrogation rooms at the County Sheriff's department. It was pretty much the same as every other interrogation room he had ever seen. Small but not cramped, dominated by a single table with four chairs. No windows, but a great big mirror; it didn't take much imagination to figure out what was on the other side or that. A single door leading to the rest of the precinct. Office. Whatever they called it out here.

It had taken the cops about twenty minutes to arrive at the house. And less than five to throw cuffs on he and Kathleen and haul them down to the station for questioning. Ronald was not a cop, sure. Never had been. But he and Kathleen did work in law enforcement...sort of. Most of the time there was a certain amount of professional consideration given between them and the cops. At least in town. Apparently not here though.

It was more than a little annoying.

"I'd rather not, no. Thanks for asking." It was probably a mistake to be a wise-ass to a guy like Barnes. Ah what the hell, he was a douchebag and Ronald was getting sick to death of the rigamarole.

Barnes' scowl grew more pronounced, and for a moment Ronald almost thought he was going to take a swing at him. Fortunately, Barnes was not a *complete* amateur. Instead of striking Ronald, he brought his hand down on the table between them with a loud SMACK. "Goddamnit, this is not a fucking game, Harper. I've got you on Breaking and Entering, Interfering with a Police Investigation..."

Ronald snorted. B&E was penny-ante shit, and they both knew it. And the other... "Hey, we called you, didn't we? As soon as we found those pictures."

"*After* you already tainted the scene. We'll be lucky to get anything useful with all the prints you two left down there." Barnes' eyes narrowed and he leaned forward in a manner that Ronald imagined was supposed to be intimidating. It just made him look stupid. "But maybe that's the point. Maybe your so-called client is your alibi, and you called us in order to deflect attention from yourselves."

He could *not* be serious. Could he?

But looking in Barnes' eyes, Ronald could see the detective meant every word he said. Inane as it sounded, he really believed he was on to something, or at least he thought he was being clever and was going to wheedle additional information out of Ronald that way.

It was too much. Ronald could not stop himself. He began to chuckle, then as Barnes' face began to flush with what Ronald could only assume was anger - it should have been embarrassment, as stupid as he was being - his chuckle became a full-on guffaw that lasted for a long couple of minutes.

The whole while, Barnes sat in silence, growing more and more red as his jaw worked. The little artery on his temple throbbed so hard the Ronald halfway expected it to burst.

"Finished?" Barnes demanded as Ronald got his laughter under control.

"I am." Ronald pushed his chair back and stood. "It's been a fun chat, but I have work to do." He began walking around the table toward the exit.

"Siddown," Barnes said. Hell, practically shouted.

Ronald stopped walking, but did not sit, instead favoring Barnes with a look that he hoped conveyed the full extent of his exasperation. "We're wasting time, Detective. I've told you everything I know. I'm sure Kathleen has done the same with your partner. Instead of continuing to beat this dead horse, we really should..."

Barnes rose suddenly, moving far more quickly and gracefully than Ronald would have given him credit for. Maybe there was more to the guy than he thought. He had Ronald by several inches, and managed to affect a somewhat effective loom. "*We* are not doing anything. You and your partner, assuming the County Attorney does not decide to press charges, are going back home and you're not going to put a foot anywhere *near* this case. We've got the ball here, and we sure don't need the likes of you meddling and hanging around underfoot." He drew in a deep breath, the air making a faint rasping sound as it entered his nostrils. "You got that, Harper?"

Ronald almost burst out laughing again, but thought the better of it. Clearly Barnes was the kind of guy who liked to think events proceeded solely the way he directed. Better to just let him have his delusions. Ronald nodded. "Got it, Detective."

Barnes looked into Ronald's eyes for a long moment. Then he gave a quick nod and gestured with his thumb toward the door. "Get the hell out of here."

RONALD SETTLED down into his desk chair and sighed contentedly. He had shopped a long time to find just the right unit for his office desk: padded without being excessively squishy, supportive without being board-like, on a swivel because… well just because, with arms long enough to comfortably rest his flesh and blood arms on and a headrest that extended above his shoulder blades. Kathleen had heckled him for a long time about how much it cost, but it was an investment worth making. That chair alone turned the days in the office into journeys to the lap of luxury. Mostly. Even better, he had caught Kathleen glancing enviously at it ever so often. She, of course, denied it.

So, despite the confusing nature of the case and the day's setback, Ronald felt quite content as he leaned back and lifted his drink - The McAllan 18, singe-malt, neat - to his lips.

"Where are we then?"

Kathleen frowned over at him from her desk - her chair was like a rock compared with his - and halfway lifted the notepad she was scanning so he could see it. "It doesn't add up," she replied. "Samuelson suspected foul play, but he didn't go to the cops…"

"Because he wanted to leave his options open for payback."

She sounded doubtful. "He looked more scared than vengeful to me." She tapped at her lip with the pen in her hand for a moment, her eyes losing focus as she drifted off into thought.

Ronald had to concede that. Only having that one meeting to go by, Samuelson did not seem the type to act hastily, or emotionally. But then again, who knows what losing a spouse will drive a man to do. If someone did something to Isabel...

Ronald gave a little jerk, almost falling out of his chair in surprise. He and Isabel had only been seeing each other for a few months, since he helped her resolve an issue with her former fiancé involving his grandmother's wedding ring. He cared about her, sure. And not just because her father was filthy rich. Hell, he had almost had to cap a couple gumbah's to protect her during that wedding ring case. But he had not really thought very deeply about how he really felt for her. The sudden possessiveness and protectiveness he just found himself experiencing was...unexpected.

Ah hell. This was not the time to lose it over some girl. There were things to do.

But then, Isabel was not just some girl, was she?

"Ah to hell with it," Ronald said, gulping down the last of his scotch - actually most of his scotch; he had not been drinking it for very long - in a single swallow. "Let's call Samuelson and get some answers out of his chubby ass."

Kathleen peered at him in silence for a moment. "The cops are probably all over him, you know."

Ronald nodded.

"We promised the Sheriff's Department we would not get any further involved in the case."

Now it was Ronald's time to give Kathleen a level, mockingly incredulous stare. She could not be serious.

Finally, after about ten seconds, she snorted out a half-laugh and grinned. "Yeah, who am I kidding, right?" She pulled open her desk drawer and pulled out the firm's address book, a thick leather-bound tome that contained contact information on all their clients, starting way back before Kathleen tempted Ronald into partnering up with her.

Very quickly, Kathleen had the book open to the "S" section. She traced down the names until she found Samuelson's, then picked up the phone from its cradle on her desk and punched in the numbers.

Fifteen seconds later, she slammed the phone down and pushed herself back from her desk forcefully enough that the rollers on her chair's legs moved her all the way back into the wall.

"Kathleen, what…"

"It's disconnected."

The words hit him like a ton of bricks. "*What?*"

"Samuelson's phone is disconnected."

Oh shit. "You don't think…"

She cut him off, nodding in the affirmative with a grim expression on her face. "We're being set up."

"SON OF A BITCH." Ronald could not believe it. But eyes do not deceive. Most of the time. Alright, some of the time.

He sat in the passenger seat of Kathleen's car, a well-maintained Chevy Malibu that sported some special modifications a mechanic friend of hers was only too happy to install. She sat behind the wheel and, like him, stared through the windshield at a large brick building that was probably once a warehouse, but now was boarded up with yellow

NO ENTRY tape strung in every doorway and window. That had not stopped people from breaking the window glass, with thrown rocks Ronald suspected. At the corner nearest them was a large sign advertising the construction project, due to start in less than a month, that would convert the old building into modern high-rent condos. Or condos anyway. Ronald was not willing to give odds what sort of rent the owners could get for them in this neighborhood.

All that was not particularly unusual or disturbing. What was disturbing was the street address of the condemned building matched the address Samuelson had given them as his place of residence.

"Son of a bitch." It bore repeating. "You sure this is the right address?"

Kathleen held up the note page where she had copied the information from the address book. 7657 Taylor Avenue. Yep, that was it. Son of a bitch.

"I don't suppose he was thinking about where he was *going* to live. You know, after the condos get built." Kathleen glowered at him and he raised his hands defensively. "Hey, just spitballing here. Son of a bitch."

"You've said that three times now, Ron."

"It's appropriate. So," he scowled deeply, "we've been had. But by whom, really? And why?" It was baffling. Ronald could not recall ever seeing Samuelson, or whoever he was, before in his life, and he had a good memory for faces and places.

"At least the cash he gave us is real."

There *was* that, at least. There are ways to test a bill to verify it is real and not counterfeit. It pained Ronald to go through the testing process, since it tended to destroy the test bills and they really needed the money; it had been a slow month at the office. But the bills passed with flying colors.

So why hire a couple of PIs for a bogus case, but pay them real money and send them to the hideout of a *real* serial killer? The pictures on the wall in the cellar, depicting body parts that had been roughly hacked off and the badly beaten faces of a number of women, sure made it seem like a killer's hideout, anyway.

"He must be trying to cover his tracks."

Ronald blinked, Kathleen's words drawing him out of his musings and back to the present. "Huh?"

Kathleen rolled her eyes slightly. "Think about it. He's accomplished what he wanted to here, and he wants to make a getaway. But the evidence is out there, and he knows it could point to him. So he cooks up a story and gets a couple of patsies to wander in to muss up the evidence. Maybe they mess it up enough to make it unusable. Maybe they do *such* a good job the cops think *they* are the killers. At the least, it delays the investigation enough for him to slip away to the next town."

Ronald shook his head. "Too many holes; the cops would quickly realize the patsies were just that. And besides, you wouldn't hire PIs for that. You'd get people who don't know what the hell they're doing."

Kathleen opened her mouth, to object Ronald was certain, but after a moment shut it again, nodding in agreement. Reluctant agreement. "In that case I've got nothing." She sighed and twisted her hands on the grip of the steering wheel. "So what now?"

"Now?" Ronald looked back at the shell of a building before them. "Now we see if we can figure out who Samuelson really is. And how he's connected to the victims in the pictures."

"That's not going to be easy. We don't even know where to start looking for him, and we don't have the pictures…"

Ronald grinned at her and pulled his cell phone, complete with its built-in high definition camera, out of his pocket. He wagged the phone back and forth and Kathleen's lips turned upward into a grin.

JOHNNY TENNEBAUM WAS in his late thirties, balding, and sported a substantial beer belly that pulled his uniform shirt tight, tight enough that Ronald always wondered why the buttons had not popped off yet. How he managed to stay on the force, as big as he was, still surprised Ronald. But he had held the position as chief evidence clerk for the local precinct for three years, and he ran a tight ship: efficient, with a perfect accountability history and not even a hint of corruption. That sort of performance from someone in such a key position probably warranted some flexibility in other re-quirements, Ronald supposed.

"Ron! How's it going, devil dog," Johnny said in greeting as Ronald entered his office, Kathleen in tow. The cop's broad grin seemed to take up his entire face. It was the kind of cheery grin that would instantly put a person at ease, make you feel welcome. Word was he had coaxed many a confes-sion out of perps with that grin, before he shifted over to the evidentiary logistics side of the world.

He never had explained, to Ronald's satisfac-tion, why he made that shift.

"Hey Johnny," Ron said, clasping hands with his friend. "You remember Kathleen?"

"Impossible to forget." Johnny winked at her

impishly, but he was harmless enough. There was no way in hell he would ever cheat on Helen. He did not want to lose his kids and most of his pension. And, Ronald was quite sure she could easily kick his ass up the street and back down again, former Marine or no.

Kathleen nodded companionably to Johnny but did not return the wink. "Do you have a moment, Lieutenant Tennebaum?" She was sometimes no fun at all.

Johnny's grin faded, his expression becoming more shrewd. "So, not a social call, huh."

"Sorry, Johnny," Ronald said, and meant it. He hated having to call in favors from friends. Or at least, he hated calling in favors that could get friends in trouble. But he saw little choice.

Johnny nodded and, turning away, gestured for them to follow him. He led Ronald and Kathleen past the caged-in desk where Johnny's duty clerks sat and maintained watch of the evidence vaults, then around the corner and into his private office. It was nothing fancy, just a simple desk in a corner and a half-dozen file cabinets against the opposite wall, but in his time on the job Johnny had made it somewhat homey. Pictures of his family sat on the desk, plaques and award citations hung on the walls, next to a big poster of his favorite Wide Receiver, and a potted fern rested in the corner nearest the door. Ronald did not want to think about the trouble Johnny had to have gone through to get approval to keep that plant in his office, let alone to keep it alive all this time.

Johnny plopped down into his chair, a simple wooden office chair on a swivel, and gestured for Ronald and Kathleen to do the same; two plain wooden chairs sat along the wall opposite the door, and caddy-corner to the file cabinets. Ronald grinned in thanks and settled down. Kathleen took a moment to close the door, earning the smallest of quirked eyebrows from Johnny, before joining him.

"What do you need, Ron?" Johnny was alway straight and to the point.

Ronald drew in a deep breath, held it for a second. This was a stretch, even considering the history he shared with Johnny. For a moment he considered forgetting the entire thing, smiling and making a joke out of it. He could certainly get a laugh out of his old friend, deflect from what was really going on... No, they needed answers. Reluctantly, Ronald push ahead.

"We need to identify some people from their photographs," he began.

Johnny looked at him askance. "That's not so hard..."

"They're dead, Johnny."

The policeman's face instantly became a mask of seriousness, his tone one of pure business. "What are you talking about?"

With a sigh, Ronald related the story of Samuelson and their trip to the house, their findings in the cellar, and their suspicions. When he was through, Johnny let out a long breath.

"Jesus, Ron." He looked away, toward one of his award citations, for a long moment before speaking again. "Look, buddy. I think you really need to leave this one alone. Let the guys up-County deal with it, and coordinate with Homicide here. They'll find this Samuelson guy, or whoever he is. No one will really think you were involved." He smiled. It was certainly intended to be a comforting smile, but it fell well short.

Ronald shook his head. "This guy decided to screw with us for a reason, Johnny. I...we...need to find out why."

Johnny frowned, but did not reply.

"Ah hell, Johnny. You know how often your boys in the force fuck things up. You've seen it. Help me out here."

Johnny's frown only grew deeper. For a few seconds there, Ronald actually thought Johnny might slap the cuffs on him and Kathleen both. Then, after what seemed an eternity, he nodded and exhaled loudly, his cheeks puffing outwards as he blew. "You got the pictures?"

Ronald gestured toward Kathleen, who opened up the small briefcase she was carrying and withdrew the prints. She handed them over and Johnny leafed through. He turned a barely-perceptible shade paler than normal as he beheld the images.

"Jesus," Johnny breathed.

"Exactly. Think your facial recognition programs can get anything off of them?"

Johnny shrugged. "Ought to." He paused, scratching at his ear for a moment. "You know the up-County homicide guys will probably send these down, if they haven't already, and our boys will run them first thing. I could just get you copies…"

"No." Kathleen was supposed to keep quiet and let Ronald do the talking. Big surprise she did not last very long in that job. Not that Ronald could blame her, necessarily. He agreed with her sentiment about not waiting.

Johnny looked between the two of them. Kathleen's jaw was set, and Ronald supposed he probably looked just as immovable as she. Finally, Johnny nodded. "Alright. I'll see what I can do. I'll call you tomorrow."

"Thanks pal." Ronald shook his hand and as always had to hold back wincing a bit at the other man's grip.

THE CALL DID NOT COME the next day, but rather two days later, at 10:30. And it was not from Johnny.

Ronald picked up the phone and recited the standard Davidson & Harper phone greeting - had to at least sound professional - and immediately wished he had not.

"Get your ass in here, Harper!" came the gruff, angry-sounding voice he knew so well. Captain Bixbie.

Ronald groaned inwardly. "Good morning, Captain," he replied with as much cheeriness as he could muster.

It didn't help.

"There will be a car out front your office in five minutes. You, and that partner of yours, will not give the officers any trouble. You're just going to get in the car with them. Understood?"

Ronald glanced over at Kathleen, who was watching from her desk, one eyebrow quirked upward curiously. He gave a little shrug and a thumbs down, and her face grew grim.

"Ok, five minutes. Looking forward to it."

Bixbie just grunted, and the line went dead.

"That what I think it was," Kathleen asked.

Ronald nodded.

"Crap."

He agreed completely.

CAPTAIN BIXBIE WAS EVERYTHING the stereo-typical Police Captain was not: lean, tall, with youthful features that did not match his age, yellow-brown hair without a trace of grey that hung to his shoulders. He was impeccably dressed in a suit that had to be taylor made, it fit him so well. His office was neat and organized, everything arranged just-so. Even the bulletin board on his wall, normally cluttered with wanted posters, announcements, or whatever, was almost severe in its lines and columns of papers. And there was not even a hint of cigarette odor in the place. Unnatural.

Ronald and Kathleen sat in padded chairs - the padding was actually halfway comfortable - across from Bixbie's cider block-shaped desk, awaiting the Captain's ire. Johnny stood at parade rest along the wall next to the bulletin board. He did not look happy.

Ronald couldn't blame him. Bixbie was legendary for his outbursts.

"Davidson and Harper," Bixbie said, his voice gravelly and disapproving. "You two have been a royal pain in my ass, you know that?"

Ronald could not help smiling. It was good to hear all his efforts had not been vain. Beside him, Kathleen shifted in her seat but kept her face smooth.

Bixbie continued, "I don't appreciate your meddling, but," His mouth twisted into something that might have been a smile, except it looked more like a sneer, "when Lieutenant Tennebaum showed me what you found... Well, I think we can let it slide this time." Why that little... Ronald had not thought Johnny would rat them out. Get caught, maybe, but not sell them out.

Wait. What did Bixbie just say?

Bixbie picked up a small remote control that lay on his desk and clicked it. A flat screen that hung on the wall to Ron's left flickered to life, and Bixbie nodded at Johnny.

Johnny came to attention, then nodded in return and turned his attention to Ronald and Kathleen. He did not even have the grace to look apologetic. "I ran the pictures you gave me through facial recognition. It took a while, but we found several matches."

He walked over to the Captain and took the remote, then clicked the button again. On the flat screen, the pictures of three women appeared. All were in their mid-30s, white, and blonde. They were best described as plain: not ugly, but not beautiful either. A few pounds overweight. And, Ronald surmised from the shape of their mouths, happy.

"These woman all disappeared in the last two years," Johnny said. "Mary Gibbons was last seen two counties over, walking her dog on a Sunday morning. Lisa Carpenter vanished from her home in Springfield last October. Her boyfriend was supposed to come over for dinner, but when he showed up, she was not there." He clicked the remote again and the first two pictures faded, leaving the last woman's image to fill the screen. "And then we have Melanie Fisher."

Johnny looked back at Captain Bixbie, who nodded before taking over the floor again. "Mrs. Fisher was reported missing by her husband, Jeremy, six months ago. You may recall the case from the news reporting."

Ronald frowned. It did not ring a bell, per say. But then, he had been rather busy when all this happened. Recovering from a gunshot wound will do that to you.

Kathleen piped up, "I remember that." She looked at the screen for a long moment, frowning.

"But I thought that case was solved. Didn't they arrest her husband, or something?"

Silence was Bixbie's only reply for several seconds. He did *not* look pleased at all.

"That's where things become interesting. Her husband was a taken into custody as a person of interest, but released after questioning." He gestured to Johnny, who clicked the remote again, and a new image appeared on the screen. "Recognize him?"

Ronald did indeed recognize the man in the picture - Samuelson.

"Son of a bitch," he said. In unison with Kathleen, who looked as stunned - as *pissed* - as he felt.

"Thought that would get your attention," Bixbie said in a wry tone. "A week after he was released, the cops up-County discovered evidence that linked all three disappearances and pointed to Fisher as the culprit behind all of them. But when they went to arrest him, he had vanished."

"You've got to be kidding me," Ronald said. "Why would he suddenly come out of hiding if he was the bad guy?"

Johnny spoke up. "That is why I brought the Captain into this, Ron. If you look a bit deeper into this case..." He shook his head, frowning. "Have you ever heard the term, orgy of evidence?"

"Sure. That's when you find all the evidence to solve the case in one fell swoop. It's quite convenient."

Kathleen snorted. "It also never really happens that way in real life."

"Exactly. But it seems that's what happened here. The homicide guys up-county all of a sudden went from nothing, only suspicion, to fingerprints, DNA evidence, hell even photographs." Johnny hit the remote again and another set of images filled the screen: tagged evidence, pdfs of coroner's reports, and photographs showing all three women in various locations - both dead and alive.

"So you're saying, what, that he was set up?"

Bixbie nodded, leaning forward in his desk. "Precisely, Miss Davidson. We did a little digging yesterday, after LT Tennebaum showed me what he found. Take a look at these pictures."

Johnny actuated the remote, and the three pictures showing the women alive expanded from the collage to fill the entire screen. All showed the women, smiling, in a park setting. Two were alone, one with a group of friends, and all appeared to be having a good time. All the same, there was something...

"Is that the same park?" As soon as Kathleen voiced the thought, Ronald realized she was correct. The three missing - dead - women had all visited the same park.

"It is," Johnny said. "And what's more, from the time stamps in the photos' metadata, they were all there on the same day."

Well, that was something. "Ok," Ronald said. "So now we know when the killer picked them out."

"We know more than that." Johnny tapped the remote again and the image of Mrs. Fisher expanded to take up the entire screen. She was sitting on the side of a small fountain that was carved in the shape of a cherub sitting atop a fish that was spitting water. Ronald's parents had a similar fountain in their yard when he was growing up; there was nothing special about it. What was he supposed to...

He saw it. Over Mrs. Fisher's shoulder, a couple was sitting on a bench on the far side of the fountain. Or at least the woman was sitting. The man was down on his knees as though proposing. There was something familiar about the man.

"Who is that?" he asked, standing up and walking to the screen. He pointed at the couple.

He could almost hear the satisfied grin on Johnny's face as he replied, "You're going to love this."

The picture zoomed in, and was reduced to pixels for a moment as the display processor adjusted. Then it cleared and the man's features became more clear. He was instantly recognizable now.

"Holy shee-it," Ronald breathed. "Is that Detective Barnes?"

"So what?" Kathleen sniffed and waved a dismissive hand. "So he happened to be in that park with his fiancé on that day. You may not like him but his presence means nothing."

"Except that's not his fiancé," Bixbie said. "She said no."

Ronald's eyebrows climbed on his head and he burst out laughing. Oh that was just awesome. "She has good judgment."

"She's also dead."

Ronald had to do a double-take on that. Was Bixbie serious? The Captain's severe expression said he was. Holy shit.

"What happened to her?" Kathleen asked.

Bixbie scowled. "After the break-up, she apparently decided to move back home to Connecticut. She had a blowout on the interstate. Flipped her car over the embankment and into the path of a sixteen-wheeler heading the other way."

Ronald winced. That was a bad way to go. Not the worst ever, but still bad. All the same, accidents happen. It sucked, and it was a horrible coincidence, but this accident did not mean anything for the case. He opened his mouth to say as much, but Johnny cut him off.

"Not at all connected, right?" One of his eyebrows quirked upward. "That's what we thought too. At first." He clicked the remote, and the images of the three murdered women came back up on the screen, along with a fourth. She could have been a sister to any of the three, she looked so similar to them. "This is Barnes' ex. Quite a resemblance, eh?"

"That does not mean anything either. There are lots of blonde women out there," Kathleen said, running her hand meaningfully through her own locks.

Bixbie nodded in agreement. "True. But just to be safe we checked out the good Detective's background. Turns out he used to own the house Fisher sent you to up-County. Lived in it with his almost-fiancé. He sold it a bit more than two years ago, after she passed away, to his cousin. Or so the county recorder's office said. But couldn't find any financial records that would correspond to a real estate sale, and his cousin has not been in the state since she joined the Air Force five years ago."

"Something smells fishy," Ronald said, earning nods of agreement from both cops.

Kathleen frowned, looking at the screen through narrowed eyes. "So you're saying Detective Barnes killed all these women and then tried to pin it on Fisher." She turned her gaze on Bixbie and Johnny in turn. "That *is* what you're saying?"

Bixbie and Johnny eyed each other for a long moment. Finally, Bixbie shrugged slightly and looked back at Ronald and Kathleen. His expression gave nothing away, but Ronald thought he detected a flash of something - rage? Indignation? - In his eyes.

"That is our theory," Bixbie said, his tone icy. "The women all bore a striking resemblance to the one who jilted him. He never got the chance to get even with her, so..." Bixbie spread his hands, his lips twisting into a sneer of distaste. "It's a little thin, but it was enough to convince Judge Hooper to grant us search warrants. We sent a team up-County to coordinate with the local authorities and investigate further. We should know more in a few days, tops." He took a deep breath, then managed a small smile. "But I wanted you to know that you had not been put through all that trouble for nothing."

Ronald swallowed, unsure how to respond. "Thanks. I guess." He glanced at Kathleen, who looked similarly poleaxed. It was not often the cops were courteous, let alone collegial, toward them. Maybe this was the start of a new, better working relationship.

Bixbie stood then and stepped around his desk. "Don't thank me. You're still a pain in my ass." He crossed his arms over his chest. He was not a particularly large man, but Ronald found himself looking at his eyes as though from a platform far beneath him, he was that good at looming. "I could lock both of you up for interfering in Police business. You know that, right?" Ronald did not trust himself to answer; the snark rose unbidden to the surface, and he was sure it would not serve them well to give voice to it. Bixbie continued, "Next time, someone comes to you with information concerning a possible crime, you bring it to us. Immediately. No delays. No investigation beforehand. *Right the hell now!*" His eyes narrowed and he looked first at Ronald then Kathleen with a gaze that would to Medusa to stone. "We clear?"

So much for collegial.

THREE WEEKS LATER, the news broke. And boy, did it break. It's not every day a policeman actually gets publicly disciplined; they most of the time closed their ranks, from what Ronald had seen. Which is why he never joined the force after the Corps. Oh, he had offers aplenty, but the power without accountability was not something he was comfortable with. And besides, it did not make sense to leave one government structured pay chart just to jump into a second one. He figured there was greater earning potential out in the real world.

Or at least, that's what he told himself.

Regardless, this was not just some public chastisement. cops almost never made the perp walk, so the media had a field day when Barnes walked his. And for a trio of homicides, no less! The reporters were going to dine out on this story for months.

Ronald clicked off the small television that sat atop one of the file cabinets in his office and leaned back in his chair, satisfied. "Not too shabby, huh?"

Kathleen hardly looked up from the paperwork she was filling out. "Don't throw your arm out of its socket patting yourself on the back. We didn't really do anything on this one."

Ronald sniffed. "Just shed light on a set of cases that was going the wrong way. Helped clear an innocent man, brought a killer to justice." He pushed the chair back and stood. "Shoot, I feel positively heroic."

Kathleen just chuckled, shaking her head slowly.

She was right, of course. All the same, it felt good to see things come to a fitting end. Ronald hoped Fisher, wherever he was, was watching that news feed. Finally he could restart his life without looking over his shoulder. That was worth a lot. And a good thing to, considering he still had a bill to pay, to cover their time and expenses.

Ron doubted they would ever see a penny of that money. Oh well.

He strode over to the coat rack near the door and donned his leather jacket, taking a moment to look around the small office. Yep, much better than being a cop.

"See you tomorrow," he said.

Kathleen grunted out a goodbye and he stepped out of the office. As the door swung shut behind him, Ronald thought he heard her laughing to herself.

Message From The Author

Thank you for reading my book. I hope you enjoyed reading it as much as I enjoyed writing it.

Every review helps an author out, so whether you loved this book, hated it, or something in between, please take a minute to tell other readers what you thought. All of the online retailers make it very easy to do, and I would really appreciate it.

Feel free to come say hi at my website or on Facebook. I always enjoy hearing from readers, especially since you all are, collectively, my boss.

I also have a weekly podcast, Story Time With Michael Kingswood, where I read stories and talk through some of the latest goings on in my world. I'd love to see you there.

Thanks again. My best to you and yours.

Warm Regards,
Michael Kingswood

Mailing List

If you enjoyed this book and would like word on new releases and special deals from Michael Kingswood, sign up for his newsletter on his website. Guaranteed to be spam-free, you can opt out at any time. And you can rest assured he will not share your information with anyone, for any reason.

https://michaelkingswood.com/newsletter-signup/

Supporting Patronage

Michael would like to invite you to become a supporting member of his website. Similar in concept to Patreon, a few dollars a month will give you access to exclusive content, and help him to focus more of his time to writing fun and exciting stories for your enjoyment.

Sign up at his website:

https://www.michaelkingswood.com/
membership/supporting-patronage/

The Champion

Veritas Morte

Story Collections

Tales Of Adventure #1

Tales Of Adventure #2

Short Story 10-Pack

A Jar Of Mixed Treats

Short Fiction

Michael has also published a number of shorter works,
links to which can be found on his website.